PATRICK

EATS HIS PEAS
and other stories

GEOFFREY HAYES

PATRICK
EATS HIS PEAS
and other stories

A TOON BOOK BY

GEOFFREY HAYES

TOON BOOKS IS AN IMPRINT OF CANDLEWICK PRESS

Look for PATRICK in A Teddy Bear's Picnic and Other Stories

An Eisner Best Publication for Early Readers Nominee 2012

Booklist Top 10 Graphic Novels for Youth

For Anne Schwartz

Editorial Director: FRANÇOISE MOULY

Book Design: FRANÇOISE MOULY & JONATHAN BENNETT

GEOFFREY HAYES' artwork was drawn in colored pencil.

Printed in Johor Bahru, Malaysia by Tien Wah Press (Pte.) Ltd.

Library of Congress Control Number: 2013931436

ISBN 13: 978-1-935179-34-4 ISBN 10: 1-935179-34-9

13 14 15 16 17 18 TWP 10 9 8 7 6 5 4 3 2 1

WWW.TOON-BOOKS.COM

PATRICK

EATS HIS PEAS

PEAS?
What did you go and make **PEAS** for? You ***know*** I don't like them.
Peas are **GOOD** for you.
They are ***not***!
Peas are little green balls of **MUSHY POISON**!

LITTLE GREEN BALLS OF MUSHY POISON... LITTLE GREEN BALLS OF MUSHY POISON...
Patrick! Act your age!

I'm not **hungry**!

Try to eat some anyway. I want you to be strong...
So **eat your peas**!

But Ma...I'll get **sick**.
Can't we skip it?
Ma?

Nuts!

Could I just eat a few?
How many is "*a few*"?

Two?
Sorry.

Then I'm not eating *any*!

Up to you.

Ma, I'm **ALL DONE**!

How *fast*! See, that wasn't so bad, was it?
No.

IT WAS EASY!
PLOP!
PLOP!

OOPS!
Goodness! It seems like most of the peas spilled into your *napkin*!
How did *that* happen?

No problem. There are plenty more in the pot.
FINE! I'll eat five!
But I'm going to do it my way!
LUM-DEE-DUM...
Patrick, what are you up to now?
Cooking!

Ketchup, jelly, stir, stir, stir...No more balls of mushy poison.

YUM!
Yuck!

Now are you going to put something in your *ice cream*?
No, Ma. It's *perfect* just the way it is.
THE END

PATRICK
HELPS OUT
Daddy, this is a good day to fly my **KITE**!
But there is no ***wind*** today.
There is ***some*** wind...
See?
OH!

It *must* be a good day for *something*!
It's a good day for *me* to do yardwork.

Me too!

I will be your *helper*!
?

Look, Daddy!

I'm a *TORPEDO*!
BAM!

PATRICK, I just raked those leaves!
Oh.
Sorry.

Here, why don't you dig up some weeds.

See...this is a weed... and this is a weed.
Got it?
Uh huh.

Daddy, are flowers weeds?
R-R-R-

I think some flowers came up by accident.

This is *not* working.

I know! You can water the flowers.

SPRITZ!
SPRITZ!

?

Are *people* flowers?

Nuts!

Here is something you can help me with.

Go turn on the water when I say "**ready**."
Okay.

NOW, Daddy?

In a moment, I'm not quite **ready**.

SPLOOSH

But you said: "**READY**."

Here, I'll get a towel for you, Daddy.
WAIT!

Hi, Ma!
Hi, honey. What's up?

I'm being a ***big help*** to Daddy.

He says to keep ***you*** company until he's done.
What are you making?
Can I ***help***?
Oy!
THE END

PATRICK
TAKES A BATH
But I don't *want* to take a bath! Can't I *skip* it tonight, Ma?
CAN'T I?
Nuts!
You'd think I was *dirty* or something!

PATRICK!
What are you
doing?
It's TOO HOT!
I'm adding more
cold, why?

That's better.

SPLASH!

BURBLE
BURBLE
BURBLE

My toys!

One day, this stuff was floating in the sea when *suddenly*...
There was a storm with **THUNDER** and **LIGHTNING**!
SPLISH!
BOOM!
GRRR!
PATRICK! ***What's*** going on in there?
Nothing.

Always *spoiling* my fun.

My goggles!

These goggles smell *funny*.

But I'll make the water smell *nice*.

Bubble bath!
PATRICK! Don't you think you've been in there *long enough*?
But I'm not **CLEAN** yet.

MY NAME IS PATRICK BROWN.
MY NAME IS PATRICK PAHNEE,
GOOD OLD PATRICK PAHNEE,
GOOD OLD PATRICK BROWN!
POP!
PATRICK!
Can't I leave you **alone** for **five minutes**?
Some water spilled on the floor **by accident**.
This wasn't **my** idea!

Ma, taking a bath made me *thirsty*. Can I have some milk?
You can have a bedtime snack *after* we clean up the bathroom.
!
Bedtime? **ALREADY!?**
You mean I ***wasted*** all this time taking that dumb bath?
Can't I stay up a ***little*** longer? Just ***tonight***?
CAN'T I, Ma?
MA!
THE END

PATRICK
GOES TO BED
"And they all lived happily ever after." The end.

Did the princess get her nose back?
Yes, it was there all along...

...Just like yours.

That was a good story. Let's make some fudge.
Maybe tomorrow.
Bedtime, sport!
Goodnight honey!
But not one bit of me is sleepy.
I'm going to stay awake all night.
DADDY! We didn't count the steps.
There are ten steps, remember?
Oh- right!

Why do I have to *sleep*, anyway?

So you'll feel *rested* tomorrow.
But I feel rested *now*!

You forgot to put your toys away.
I might *need* them.
Where is Happy Joe?

Not here.
Not here.

HERE HE IS!

GOOD OLD
HAPPY JOE!
H.J.

He was asleep under the pillow!

Yes, Happy Joe has been playing all day...

And now he is SLEEPY.

...

HEY! Don't open the window!

I only opened it a *crack*.
But *something* might come in.
Here, I'll put your *night light* on.
Sweet dreams.
WHOOSH!
DADDY!

Happy Joe saw a **GHOST** coming in the window!

That's not a ***ghost***. It is the ***wind***.

Nothing to fear.
Happy Joe was afraid...

I was **BRAVE**!

Then good night, ***brave sir***!

Good night.

Happy Joe, Papa says we have to go to **sleep**...

...even if we are **not** sleepy...

THE END

ABOUT THE AUTHOR

GEOFFREY HAYES, the recipient of the ALA's prestigious Theodor Seuss Geisel Award, has written and illustrated more than forty children's books, including the extremely popular series of early readers *Otto and Uncle Tooth.* But Geoffrey's most beloved creations are the Benny and Penny TOON books and the Patrick stories.

While there's some of Patrick in all of us, we can see a great deal of Geoffrey in him. Geoffrey says: "When I was six or seven, peas really did seem like 'little green balls of mushy poison.' Oddly enough, peas are now one of my favorite vegetables. Chilled pea soup with mint—that's simply delicious!"

TIPS FOR PARENTS AND TEACHERS:

HOW TO READ COMICS WITH KIDS

Kids *love* comics! They are naturally drawn to the details in the pictures, which make them want to read the words. Comics beg for repeated readings and let both emerging and reluctant readers enjoy complex stories with a rich vocabulary. But since comics have their own grammar, here are a few tips for reading them with kids:

GUIDE YOUNG READERS: Use your finger to show your place in the text, but keep it at the bottom of the speaking character so it doesn't hide the very important facial expressions.

HAM IT UP! Think of the comic book story as a play and don't hesitate to read with expression and intonation. Assign parts or get kids to supply the sound effects, a great way to reinforce phonics skills.

LET THEM GUESS. Comics provide lots of context for the words, so emerging readers can make informed guesses. Like jigsaw puzzles, comics ask readers to make connections, so check a young audience's understanding by asking, "What's this character thinking?" (but don't be surprised if a kid finds some of the comics' subtle details faster than you).

TALK ABOUT THE PICTURES. Point out how the artist paces the story with pauses (silent panels) or speeded-up action (a burst of short panels). Discuss how the size and shape of the panels carry meaning.

ABOVE ALL, ENJOY! There is of course never one right way to read, so go for the shared pleasure. Once children make the story happen in their imagination, they have discovered the thrill of reading, and you won't be able to stop them. At that point, just go get them more books, and more comics.